Dreams Come True

JAYADEVI SUNDARARAJAN

CONTENTS

1 THE WOMAN IN THE BLUE DRESS I

It was raining outside. I lay in my bed listening to the pitter-patter. There was a faint knock on the door. I got up and opened it. There was a woman at my doorstep, fainted. I looked left and right in the dark. There was no one else. Then I heard a gunshot. I quickly pulled her in and closed the door. I knelt down to look at her. She was wearing a blue dress. Suddenly she woke up, jumped up and said, "Tristan! Thank God, I've found you." Before I could tell her that I was not Thrish... Trit.. or whatever, she pressed some buttons on her strange watch, and the world around us changed. The beauty fell into my arms and said, "We are safe!" I heard a noise and turned around to look. He looked exactly like me. She looked from him to me in shock. He opened fire, and I woke up. My hand was swollen red. Then I realized it was due to a radiator burn from the previous day, and not from some ultra- thermal firing weapon.

2 THE WOMAN IN THE BLUE DRESS II

I was checking the output of IC 7842, and the results weren't quite what I had expected. It was giving me a migraine. I thought I heard a strange noise behind me and turned around. There she stood, my woman in the blue dress.

"I know this is too sudden for you, but I don't have any time to explain. Please come with me."

She grabbed my arm and punched buttons on her watch. The room changed. We were in the wilderness. All around were clusters of trees and wild ferns were growing everywhere.

"Tristan is dying. Only way I can save him is if I can retrieve what is stored in the mansion at the edge of this forest. I need Tristan to access the mansion, we need his retinal scan. You will be able to pass it. I want you to go into the mansion and obtain the box in the centre of the hall. I will cover for you from afar. People are expecting Tristan to show up here. Now go. Follow this path. Hurry."

I didn't seem to have much choice. I hurried. I heard shots behind me. I doubled and kept running. More shots behind.

There stood the white mansion. I peered into what seemed to be the eyehole. There was a click and the door opened. I entered into a huge white hall, in whose center was a single table, upon which rested a two-inch cube sized box. Without another thought, I picked it up, ran back out the door, back up the path.

No shots now. I soon came upon my woman, except she was propped up against a huge fern. She was hit and was bleeding profusely.

She said, "Good. Now listen carefully. Take my watch. Wait for the sun to go down. Then press 4862 on the watch. You will be transported to Zircov. You will recognize him immediately from his special eyes. I have to rest for a day or two."

She took off her watch and entrusted it to me.

"Now I have to butterfly.."

Instantly she disappeared. On the fern though, now sat a pretty yellow butterfly. I sat there looking at it. The light dimmed, the sun had gone out. I pressed 4862.

The scene changed. I was in a moderate sized room. I saw someone on the floor. Blood was pouring out of his riddled chest onto the floor. I drew near. The eyes were open. The irises were pure yellow.

There was a laugh behind me, I turned and looked at myself. He opened fire.

I woke. I couldn't see anything.

"You're in the hospital. You were badly wounded in the accident last night when you were driving. You've just had your left eye replaced. Lucky for you we had a donor right on time. Rest now."

Days passed. My bandages were removed. I opened my eyes. There had been a powerful fragrance emanating from my right all these days. I turned to my right. I saw a bouquet of beautiful flowers in a vase, and hovering over the flowers was a heart-warming yellow butterfly.

They handed me a mirror hesitantly. I looked. My left eye had an iris that was lemon yellow.

3 THE WOMAN IN THE BLUE DRESS III

I was walking in the sand, listening to the waves. She appeared out of nowhere. She looked distraught with anxiety, out of control. "Tristan's dying and it's all my fault!" with that she broke into tears, and walked hither and thither. I motioned her to the higher ground on the beach that lent itself like a parapet. She gave up and went and sat down. She cried for a while and then calmed down. "Would you like something to drink?" She nodded.

I went to the house, and found the fresh coffee l had brewed for the evening. I poured her a cup, added cream and sugar, like I did to my own coffee. Somehow, I knew, that was how she liked it too. On my way out, my eyes fell on the highly ornate kerchiefs I had bought for my sister's birthday present. "She can wait," I thought to myself. I grabbed them with my free hand.

She was sitting there quietly hugging herself. I sat down beside her not wanting to disturb her reverie. She saw what I had brought, she gently picked a kerchief from my hand on my lap, and brushed her face. A cold wind blew just then, I put the hot cup in her hands, hoping it would warm her. She breathed, and was lost, looking unfocussed at the cup's contents. I waited as she slowly recovered and took occasional sips.

We were quiet for a while. It was getting dimmer. The change in the light must have somehow affected her, for she broke out again suddenly. I hesitated for a second, got up and knelt on one knee before her, reached my hand and touched her cheek, "It's Okay. It's going to be okay." She looked down and stilled her mind, and let it be for a while. She fingered the rims of her watch, and looked up at me. I held her eyes as tenderly as I could, as she brought herself to click the watch.

She was sitting on a bench, and behind her was a glass wall, on the other side of which lay Tristan on a white bed, with medical equipment strewn all around. "It's okay Lizine, we found a donor match." I turned to see a white-haired doctor. She ran up to the white wall, and was shaking in tears. I walked to her and rested my hand on her shoulder. She turned around, and worked her watch.

The beach had darkened. She cried into my arms forever till she was too weak. I carried her to the house, and laid her on my bed. She fell asleep almost instantly. Good thing I had laundered the sheets in the morning. I pulled an arm-chair close to her. She seemed drained out. Then I noticed her watch was playing a light sequence, and she zapped(disappeared). The watch must have detected her sleep cycle rhythm, and transported her to her Secure room. Tristan's idea, possibly.

I walked to the other side of the bed, and lay myself down.
I let my breath out, and let my body relax.

4 THE WOMAN IN THE BLUE DRESS IV

I was walking slowly, almost standing on a square tower full of people. I could hear Tristan's voice goading the people to cheer. I walked a little bit, and could see him, fitted with a large amount of gold, his arms up in the air as he gave his vigorous speech. Then, I noticed her. Lizine was sitting down one chair away from Tristan's chair. Between their chairs sat an elegant woman dressed in gold. Lizine was dressed in green, not much jewellery. It occurred to me suddenly that Lizine wasn't Tristan's first love interest. Lizine may not be his love interest at all! There was something in her face; she was listening and looking devoutly on Tristan. She was in love, but it wasn't being matched by him!

Later, Lizine found me.
Lizine asked, "How did you get here?"
I said, "I can't seem to remember"
I heard Tristan's voice behind me, "I had him brought here for Zircov's trial!"
My vision was blurring. I could hear Tristan's laughter. I lost consciousness.

My head was clearing. A few men were punching me.
"So, we heard people from alternate universes are trespassing our space. This one looks just like Tristan."
"This the one Lyzine has a soft spot for?"
"Yeah, yeah"
 He took out a knife and punched my stomach!
Aaaah!

I woke up. I was lying on a bench. There were people moving around everywhere. Everyone wore grey dresses. There were lines of people at counters. Cafeteria? Then I saw uniformed soldiers with guns! I tried to sit up and succeeded. I looked down, and saw a heavy iron ball chained to my leg! I was in a prison!

My sister was visiting me. "What happened to me?" She said, "You came to my birthday party. But you looked like a Zombie. You just went to a chair and sat there for hours. It was very unlike you. You wouldn't talk to any one of us. I thought maybe you needed rest, you were tired and preoccupied. I cut the cake, and fed my fiance. He fed me. He turned around, and you stabbed him with the kitchen knife. Luckily you missed his heart."

5 THE WOMAN IN THE BLUE DRESS V

I was in my cell, and Lizine appeared with someone that looked just like me and Tristan, only he was clothed just like me. "He is a robot. He is programmed to behave like you." "Can he eat like me?" "Yes. And his stomach can make the food disappear in its anti-matter cavity." "Come with me", she fingered her watch.

We were in a meeting room. Everyone looked solemn. "I want you to help me assassinate Tristan." "What!?"

--

It was all over. She smiled at me. And then, she shot me!

--

I woke up on the beach sand. Lizine appeared out of thin air. "The watch doesn't work well. It refuses to teleport you back. Some virus." She knelt down. "I don't know what's gonna happen next. Tristan's friends will find a way to hunt us down. We did the right thing though. People have been saved. And there are people, lots of them, on our side too."

She smiled and said, "I'm so bored now!" I laughed. The sun was scorching, but it still felt nice on the skin, after days of prowling in the dark. We could hear the waves washing up on the sand. Slowly we discerned people on the beach a little farther away. It was a public spot. Children were playing frisbee, flying kites, playing fetch with their dogs. People sitting under umbrellas, and chatting away. "Are you hungry?" "Yes." We walked our way to my beach house hand-in-hand. "Just apples in the fridge." "Apples will do." I took out a steel plate, washed the apple and knife, cut the apple in half, cut off the centre, top and bottom of the halves and peeled the skin. I pulled out two small plates, put half an apple on each, and sliced the halves. I handed one plate to Lyzine (also spelt Lizine or Lyceine) and took the other. We sat at the dining table, eating apple slices quietly. "So, tell me a little about yourself", I said. She laughed.

6 THE WOMAN IN THE BLUE DRESS VI

We were back on the beach. Just standing there. When a little further away someone emerged out of thin air, gun pointed towards us! I reached down to my boots, pulled out a knife and threw it at him accurately. He zapped! How did it happen? How did I know there was a knife in my boot & how did I throw it accurately, almost like a reflex action?

Lizine said, "You are remembering your previous life. I had some memories wash over me sometime too. You always protected me in your previous life."

I said, "This place is not safe, Lizinel"

She punched her watch and the beach around us gave way to a compact room.

Lizine said, "This is my home away from home. Tristan has never been here. No one can know."

"I think the virus in your watch is letting them follow us!"

"Didn't think of that. I have another teleporter watch stored in the drawer. I'll switch to that one and we can leave immediately. But where to?"

"I think we can go to my sister's place. How can we get the coordinates?"

She fingered the watch, and a ray of light flashed on my face.

"Think of her place."

I did. Numbers appeared on her watch screen. She punched those numbers.

"Hope this works."

The compact room changed to a spacious living room.

The wall clock said 2 am. My sister came out of a neighbouring room.

"Adrianna!"

"Paul, how did you get here? Fred is sleeping. Let's go upstairs."

"Did she get you out of prison?"

"Yes. Adrianna, can you get something to eat?"

"Sure."

Lizine and I went upstairs. I let out a deep breath and turned to Lizine. She looked very tired. I tucked her hair back and cupped her face with my hand, and looked into her eyes that seemed to say a million things all at the same time, that none of them were intelligible.

We heard footsteps coming up on the stairs. Momentarily my sister appeared with sandwiches, which we were very thankful for. Adrianna asked, "So what's happening?" I tried to tell her the whole story so far, she listened intently. Adrianna said, "I don't know if you have been hallucinating or if this is real, I don't know if I should call the cops or the asylum. You seem too crazy!" And then it happened, my hands were disappearing! I looked towards Lizine and her hands were disappearing too! I looked at Adrianna, nothing was happening to her. But she looked like she was in a nightmare! Soon both of us disappeared. And then it happened, the room and Adrianna dissolved and we were in an open space surrounded by thick jungle.

I looked at Tristan practicing throwing knives at a dartboard! He looked at me and I instinctively pulled a knife from the left boot and threw it at him. Bang on target. The hand he had raised to throw at me fell, and then he zapped! Then, I heard my name called, "Paul!" I was like, "Mom!" I turned to my 10 O'clock and saw my mum and dad standing!

Mum asked, "Did you eat plums from Adrianna's garden?" I said, "I don't know. We might have." The sandwiches had plum jam, I thought. Mum said, "We were eating plums and we disappeared in front of Adrianna's eyes and came here seven years ago." I said, "I thought you were travelling the world and met with an accident. That's what Adrianna had told me." Mum said, "Yes, oh well. Few hours back this Tristan appeared looking like you.." We had buried Tristan, and yet he must have zapped and appeared here. In this Universe. What was this place, heaven? I was suddenly worried about Adrianna. "Mum, Adrianna?" "We have a tv that telecasts her living room 24 x 7". Mum led the way to the tv, and we saw Adrianna in the couch crying terrified tears. But she was safe.

"Lizine, can you take us all back there?" "We can try." "Mom! Dad! hold hands together." I put one hand on Lizine's waist and another held my mum's hand. Lizine punched and the jungle gave way to Adrianna's living room.

Adrianna looked up through watery eyes, sandwich in one hand. "No, don't eat that sandwich!" all four said. Her hand dropped it to the floor. We heard Fred stirring in the next room! Drowsy eyed he opened the door.

We sat him down, and I explained my side of the story in short. "I'm an accountant, but how do you expect me to understand and believe all you've just said?!" Fred said. My sister nodded her head many times during the explanations though. I took it as a good sign. Mum and Dad looked thrilled, nothing surprised them though. Finally, Adrianna said, "There's chappatis in the Fridge. Sag paneer and channa masala. Let's eat!"

7 THE WOMAN IN THE BLUE DRESS
VII

Tristan took Lizine's watch at gunpoint. Tristan said, "We've rigged this whole place with dynamite. Have fun."

Everything was blowing up afar. I held Lizine tightly, and focused intently on our beach, with my eyes closed shut.

I opened my eyes, and saw we were on the beach! "Tristan! Paul! you did it. You are capable of teleporting through universes at will if you really want it! I have read about this, but never seen it happen. And you can do it!"

"Are you telling me you didn't use your watch?"

"No, I didn't use my watch!"

"Maybe your watch got set to auto mode."

"No, I don't have any watch on me."

"Someone could have teleported us..."

"I felt you teleport us."

"Really?"

"Yes!"

"Why did you call me Tristan?"

"I just liked the name Tristan. Can I call you Tristan?"

"Sure, Lizine. Anything you like," I said and smiled at her.

"I want to call our daughter Simona" she said!

I laughed and held on to her.

8 THE GIRL IN THE PINK DRESS I

"Hi! My name is Simona, and I've come to take you home."

I had been stranded on this planet for weeks with no memory. But I felt peace within. And a sadness. But now,

"Simona, honey, let's get home." We willed our way to home.

Lizine said, "We found out that they had taken you by force, and tried to obliterate your memory, and put in Tristan's memories in you. But you escaped in a pod, and steered it with your will into a different universe."

Simona said, "It's hard to obliterate memories, Daddy. Especially funny ones. I read about this in a book."

Lizine said, "Simona had dreams everyday of you on a green planet, and in every dream, you told her a new paraprosdokian."

Paraprosdokians are figures of speech in which the latter

part of a sentence or phrase is surprising or unexpected and is frequently humorous.

Lizine continued, "The ones you created for your friends. We have it noted down, all of them. Here!"

I read them.

> *'Grass is always greener if you wear green cooling glasses.*
>
> *Grass is always greener if you turn up the color on your tv.*
>
> *As easy as pie, but I can't reach the end of that number.*
>
> *Knowledge is power, but not in an outage.*
>
> *Everything dies, except my hair. Tried all kinds of dyes.*
>
> *"Will you marry me?" "Yes, I'll marry Mi." (Stan is proposing to Emily, and Mi is their common friend.)'*

I said, "These are great, I do remember them."

Lizine was all tears, "You get your memories back, if you meet your loved ones. You met Simona, and everything came back to you. Adrianna, Fred, Mom and Dad are in the next room."

Lizine continued, "Simona kept asking me if she could go fetch you. I kept saying no. But, the paraprosdokians kept reassuring us. And one day, I braved it, I told Simona that she could try and go to you. You know, she's a natural like you, travelling through spaces. But, in between universes, I just didn't know. She is so young, and yet I didn't know if this green planet possibly in a different universe was reachable to her or not."

I said, "It's okay, Lizine. It's okay. I'm here now."

We had a space net around our city, that allowed only individuals with memory imprint of this place to univport or teleport in. So, we felt safe for now. Lizine was not going to let me travel out of the city for now, I could tell.

I said, "There were sufficient apple trees, on the green planet."

Lizine smiled.

I said, "I think it was the garden of Eden, where I first met you."

Lizine said, "You are kidding, right?"

I said, " Yeah! ofcourse I'm kidding." and smiled at her. Simona, the girl in the pink dress, was smiling.

9 THE GIRL IN THE PINK DRESS II

Lizine had ordered a Virtual Reality head-set kit for Simona, that took you to scuba dives across many seas and oceans, and you could view colorful shoals of fishes swimming all around you. "These views are really nice, Daddy. It's like being inside the ocean."

Lizine said, "Put them away for a while, Simona."

Lizine said to me, "Maybe this VR thing is not such a good idea.   She is always very tired afterwards."

I said, "Simona, come here. I want to show you some of the poetry I wrote, when I was alone at the beach house, when I had met Mommy just twice."

Simona picked up the notebook from my table, and started reading aloud the following poem I had scribbled:

Don't be rash

On his forehead was ash
For his birthday bash
They gave him some cash
Out the door did he dash

On his head was a deep gash
Blood dripping on his eye-lash
His neck in a whiplash
Some dreams of his went smash

On his hand was IV rash
The doctors got their stash
If only he hadn't been rash
He'd be at his party with a splash!

Simona said, "Dad, this is nice! I like it." She went on to another piece of my work:

Time-out Min

He took out the trash bin,
Children outside causing a din
He felt like a fish with no fin,
Poured himself some gin.

He took out his anger on his kin,
Shouted keep the radio on min,
Wife searching where's my pin,
Chased him out to buy some rin.

He took out his list of sin,
Just want a day at Holiday Inn,
Don't want to wear himself thin,
Only way to get all to win!

Simona said, "Wow! Dad, you remembered your punctuations this time! But what is Rin, and Holiday inn? Explain it to me." And so, I did. She wanted to read one more. It was late for bed, but I let her read one more:

<u>*Light the match*</u>

She got out her cookie batch,
Tossed one to him to catch,
Onto it did he latch,
Forgot about the cricket match.

She got out onto a grassy patch,
Walked on to get the satch,
From the barn she did snatch,
The mud floor she did scratch.

She got her hair in the thatch,
Now flying she rode to match,
His car speed wearing an eye patch,
A new plan did they hatch!

"Do you know how I wrote these, Simona?" "Go on, tell me Daddy." And I told her. She was happy with what I said, and feel asleep on the sofa.

Next day was Sunday. Simona was free to go anywhere in the city for a few hours in the morning. Lizine made her favorite breakfast, bread with apple jam. Simona took off on her bike.

In a few seconds, I got a phone call from city security. "Paul, I saw the space net logs yesterday, since unusually large amounts of information were being sent out of the city. These contain visuals of Simona's memories!". I said,

"Deactivate Simona_in!"

I called Lyzine, Adrianna, Fred, Mom, Dad and her best friend Pierre on an instant video call. The screen sprang up from my watch in front of me. "If you see Simona, ask her what is special about my poetry. This is important! The correct answer is: The rhyming words in my poems are in almost alphabetical order! Report back as soon as you can." The real Simona was with Pierre. We rounded up all the other Simona robots in a thorough search of the city.

Lyzine said, "Explain to me!". I held her shoulders with both hands and said, "Lyzine that VR kit was rigged. It was scanning Simona's brain and sending out her memories! The space net scans physical appearance, and memories to allow univport or teleport in. Tristan's been orchestrating Simona robot attacks! He put Simona's transmitted memories in robots, Lizine, and they got through space net into the city. Luckily, he didn't bomb the city using the robots. He still wants the city to himself, and his robots lack attacking tactics. He was probably trying to get more information on the city."

10 THE GIRL IN THE PINK DRESS Z

Tristan said, "You'll never find Simona again! I've expunged her!" I was about to explode his ship from our ship's blaster, but his ship had univport tech, and vanished instantly. I wouldn't have blasted his ship. Tristan might have lied. Simona might have been on that ship. But, everyone knew, Tristan never lies. But, I, never take a chance. I, am very thorough. Find Simona first, Tristan can die later.

I looked at Lizine, and said, "When you want to escape, you steer to the happiest safest place you remember at that moment. I think Simona went to the green planet. She was there to save me, she felt happiest in that moment." I hugged Lizine and univported us to the green planet. There she was! Our doll! "Oh, Simona!", Lizine knelt and hugged her. I kept watching. Simona was looking at me.

"You didn't want to spook Mommy. But it *was* Eden. And I was an angel watching over you!" I laughed. "Sure, you were!" At that moment, I felt content. I could even forgive Tristan. As long as he stayed away.

11 THE GIRL IN THE PINK DRESS Z1

I was saying to Lizine, "I spent some time looking at the VR kit, and the memory transmissions in the logs. The VR kit was programmed to read all her memories, her entire brain. But, from the log, only memories of her textbooks, and scenic views of the city were there. No memory of Pierre, or any of us was in the log. You know what this means? Simona was subconsciously fighting the VR kit. Her brain was refusing to give-up personal memories. It was interacting with the VR kit!

There's another shocking thing I discovered. She was transmitting memories of her standing in front of the mirror. It was like she was taunting Tristan. Almost threatening him.

After the robot attacks, I had installed personnel supervision of people coming into the city. It was impossible for Tristan to enter the city, to kidnap Simona. I suspect after school she went out of space net, and appeared on Tristan's radar on purpose! We have to talk to her,

Lizine. She can't do things like this." Lizine's face was pale, she wasn't looking at me. I turned to look, and Simona was standing there.

"Daddy, I had a vision of Tristan's ship disappearing. It's tech we don't have. I didn't think it right for Tristan to have power like that. When I was on his ship, I reached out with my mind, and read its design. I know how to build a ship like that now. Also, when he moved the ship, I sent it to the Sahara. Just before exiting his ship, I programmed the computer to override his co-ordinates and shutdown itself irreparably after reaching Sahara."

The Sahara was a desert planet, at the far end of the galaxy, with very little vegetation, and no known civilizations.

"Don't worry about Tristan, Daddy. Tristan is clever, he will fix his rig. But it will take him some time."

"Come here Simona", and I hugged her.

"We can't have him going to places, and blasting people out there, Daddy!"

Lizine fainted. We splashed water on her face, and revived her. We let here rest in her room.

In the living room, I asked, "Simona, where were you on his ship? He said he expunged you."

"I was in the incinerator, Daddy. That's where I read the

ship's design."

"That's too risky, Simona. Too risky."

"But I got out of there before he turned on the switch."

"You don't have to tell mom this. Not unless she asks you."

"Ok, Daddy."

"Simona, I have been working on a project to shut down the pathways between universes. You want to take a look?"

"Oh! that's wonderful, Daddy!", she jumped up, and hugged me. There is always more than one way to solve a problem. I had to teach Simona that.

Lizine called out, "What are you two up to?"

Simona said, "We're reading poetry mother."

"Which ones?"

"Timeless thoughts by Jay."

"Oh, okay."

We grabbed the book from the shelf, and headed to Lizine. Simona read aloud

these poems:

Timeless thoughts

by Jay

Love

An island and an oasis
*   are in love*
the stars in the sky
*   are playing messengers*

Hope

We are all connected

We are all one

You and I, we can

Never come undone.

Saving

In the darkness of my soul

You set ablaze a raging wild fire

I surrender and surrender

Flames are now dying down

You quench it with your smile

Ray of light comes through

As I walk towards you

Cool breeze blows

Everything slows

Tender leaves appear on stems

You breathe life into my very being.

Life

This body is fragile
It will disappear one day
Yet we live like
We exist forever way.

You

I tremble afraid to lose what I have

I stumble upon all my banes

I fumble everything

I tumble upon the plains

I reach out and cry

My tears have run dry

You come as a balm

And I fall asleep.

Lizine smiled and fell asleep. We wandered into the living room. We were silent for a long time.

"I liked the poems," Simona said, "Let's go to work, Daddy."

"Alright."

We were in my hobby room. I showed Simona how there are specific pathways between universes, and how we can identify them.

"You have been monitoring the inter-universe pathways, haven't you, Daddy?"

"Yes."

"As many as you can?"

"Yes."

"Cause there would possibly be infinite pathways."

"Yes."

"And there has been no traffic?"

"No traffic since the time I've been tracking. How'd you guess?"

"Just a feeling, Daddy."

"Lizine's watches were created by Zircov. But, he's dead. I don't think there are many out there that are aware of such tech."

"Hm."

"Let's take a break. Do you want to read some jokes?" Simona nodded. I pulled out these from an old book:

At a textile processing plant:

"When will you dye? "
"Not too soon I hope"

At the bar:

"Do you have any ice? "
"Yes, two"

At the ice cream parlor:

"How many sundaes did you sell this week?"
"Only one as ever "

At the kitchen:

"There is no rise in the oven. "
"There is some in the cooker. "

At a departmental store:

"I need some spice. "
"We don't sell spies. "

At this page:

"Did you get the punch? "
"Sure did" and punches my face!

Simona laughed! I smiled. Lizine stood at the doorway, not smiling exactly.

"Bad dreams?" I asked.

"Sort of." Lizine said.

I said, "We shouldn't have read you heavy poetry before your sleep. Come hear these jokes?"

Lizine walked over slowly, and plopped on the couch. We read some more jokes. Lizine was slowly smiling. Simona leaned on her. I thought, "this is a dream I don't ever want to wake up from."

12 THE BOY IN THE BROWN DRESS I

He was kissing a girl, when Simona drove up to school. Simona was shocked.

"Bye Julie. My mom's here." Julie smiled. Aaron jumped into the passenger front seat of the convertible. Simona drove, and then stopped by the park on the way to their house.

She then said to him, "Aaron you are just fourteen, and you are already kissing a girl??"

"It's alright Mom, I'm going to marry her someday. But, hey, listen, I've got to tell you something. Some of my dreams are from the future. Last month, I had a dream about this exact moment. I dreamt this exactly, me kissing Julie, and you driving up in the convertible. I didn't even know her much then. But, in less than a month, I got to know her, we are lab partners in digital signal processing, and we keep finishing each other's sentences. We seem to know exactly what the other person is thinking."

Simona said, "Well, I'm more of the opinion that this in an adolescent crush and too much chemistry, hormones or whatever. It's too early to be talking about marriage. And definitely way too early for kissing. It's not hygienic, that's what I think. I can't believe I'm having this conversation with you!"

"No mom, seriously, it's just kissing. I promise we won't go further, without a few years passing by."

Simona looked like she was having a sinking feeling in the pit of her stomach.

They drove in silence. Later that day, Simona found me, and said, "Dad, Aaron is saying he is getting dreams of or from the future." I asked, "Anything serious?" "No Dad, it sounded like a one-off dream from the future. Should we be worried? Should I ask him more?" I said, "I don't think we need to panic, Simona. Tell me more details, I'm sure Aaron is mature, and will tell us if there is anything to worry."

I woke up. Lyceine was sleeping beside me. And Simona was sleeping across the hall in her bed. We slept with Simona in the same room. Simona never wanted a separate room. What kind of dream was this? Simona, a mom? She is just sixteen now, and she was all grown up in the dream! And I saw Simona and Aaron talk, when I wasn't even in the scene. But, how could this be. I felt like a ghost then, but I felt like myself, when I was taking to Simona. My mind might be overworked, and I could have dreamt it out of anxiety for Simona's future. But somehow I felt like this dream is going to come to pass. This might be a dream of the future, and Aaron the boy in the brown dress, would he inherit this power of dreaming about the future from me?

After breakfast, I was lounging in the chair, and Simona was lying stomach down on her bed, elbows propping her up, pencil in hand, and a book and notebook open in front of her. She said, "Dad, if I get a son, I'll name him Aaron, and if I get a daughter, I'm naming her Andrea. That way they will always be on the top of the list everywhere. They'll get alphabetical order supremacy," and she smiled.

I was aghast. Simona said, "Dad, don't take it seriously. I love my name. Just Simona is way down the list, a little uncomfortable for procedures like roll call or scanning the list of marks on the bulletin, but I don't have serious complaints. Please don't feel bad Dad! On second thoughts, it's going to be Aarti instead of Andrea. Aarti would put her more near the top of the list."

How was I to tell her I was shocked that she was thinking of the name Aaron for her son!

13 THE BOY IN THE BROWN DRESS II

Aaron wakes up and finds Lyceine and Adrianna conversing. What a dream he had had. Aaron has a strange expression on his face. Lyceine asks, "What is it, Aaron?" Aaron says, "I just had a dream. Julie and I were walking in a desolate place, and suddenly she was struck by lightning. She charred like a wooden doll, and her arms, legs, trunk were scattered. I quietly picked them up, and carried them over my head, like I knew how to put her back together and bring her back to life." Lyceine and Adrianna looked at each other. Lyceine said, "It's probably all those videos you were watching yesterday. Something about fire, wasn't it?" Aaron says, "Yeah, probably."

I woke up looking aghast. Can I dream about Aaron talking about his dream? And his dreams come true? That's just.. It can't be. This gruesome dream can't come true. Probably only some of his dreams come true.

Simona, "Dad, what happened?"

Me, "Just a weird dream Simona."

Simona, "Tell me about it."

Me, "Maybe another day."

Simona, "Okay, you rest now."

I felt like my head could do nothing. I didn't know how to come out of this feeling. I closed my eyes and drifted into a dreamless sleep. When I woke up, Lyceine had made me my favorite food, apple pancakes with apple jam. Simona showed me something Pierre had been writing for her. It was incredibly romantic.

> *'I'm at the coffee club, just sitting in the chair sipping coffee, and looking at you and smiling. It's a beautiful feeling. The aroma of the coffee is so fine. It puts me in a good mood. I lean across the table and take your hand in mine. You smile.*
>
> *I wake up, the sun is streaming in softly through the window. You are at your desk writing with a cup of tea on the table. I sit up. You turn and smile at me. What a way to begin the day.*
>
> *We are walking together, with dim streaks of light peeping through the clouds. Our hands are together, and we are so aware of being with each other. We steal glances of each other, catch each other's eyes occasionally, and keep smiling. Thought crosses the mind, that we don't want this to ever end. We could spend a lifetime here, like this.*
>
> *Let's pack up and leave. Run away to the end of the universe, where no one troubles us. Just you and me in peace.*

Maybe a few kittens.

Dew drops on the green grass glistening in the morning sun. Little flowers spotting on the grass here and there. There is a brown round wooden table, and a little wooden chair. I sit on it. Children running around. I wait for you to come. Something is holding you back. I understand. But I live here anyways, knowing the universe connects us."

Pure love is hopeful. Unafraid of separation. Completely with the belief of being together always.

I was at peace. I closed my eyes. I reached with my mind. What would Aaron do with the charred pieces? He placed them together on a long table, exactly as they would fit together to form Julie. He put his hands on her head, closed his eyes and sensed. Yes, there still was brain activity. She was still there. He reached out to her softly with his voice, "Wake up, Julie." A soft glowing light was passing from his hands to her head, and slowly it spread down her shoulders, trunk, hands and arms. Inside her brain Julie was thinking random thoughts of leaving to a different world, but she heard Aaron's voice, "Stay with me, Julie. I need you here." There was a pull to the other world, it felt too easy to let go, but Aaron's voice kept reaching her, "Julie, you can heal yourself. You can operate at cellular level. You can mesh your body together. You can come alive. It's possible." Something within her changed. She could feel her limbs. Something warm was flowing through her, and then something cool was flowing through her. Her heart started pumping. Blood coursed through her veins like water through a dried plant, and she rejuvenated like that plant. She slowly opened her eyes. Aaron slowly let go of her head. He put his hands on the table and breathed heavily.

I opened my eyes. Aaron had healing hands.

14 THE WOMAN IN THE PURPLE DRESS I

Andrea was saying to Pierre, "Father, you know how my friend Anita and I are fond of Hindu mythology. I've written something I'd like you to read. Remember how Anita was telling us Draupadi's story the other day. I've based it on that." Pierre read as follows,

"Trailer – Mahabharat 2100

Extract from Mahabharat 2100

Denesia was developed using synthetic DNA. The body breathed and the brain had no memories. Denesia was about twenty-five years old. Her creator prayed to _his_ creator devotedly, and He appeared and granted him his wish. For Denesia to wake up, with a certain amount of knowledge, and He gifted Denesia three blue crystals that adorned a necklace for her. He said, as long as there is one crystal left,

Denesia will keep living. So, Denesia woke, and was thrilled, and amazed, of her surroundings.

She married the five brothers of Peter — Yvonne, Brandon, Aden and the twins. Nion came to her after the wedding, and promised to be her friend.

Nion and Denesia were on a hilltop, when Nion saw there was some problem with the planet in the sky, it was about to explode! He uses his mind energy to contain the explosion of the planet, so that debris of the explosion doesn't harm earth. But the effort leaves Nion very weak, and he says, "I may have to leave this body. My purpose for this incarnation has not yet been fulfilled, but I must make allowances for bug in planetary management." Denesia is scared. She pulls away a crystal from her necklace and puts it in Nion's hand, and closes his fist. Nion absorbs the energy of the crystal, and sits up, a little fatigued, but feeling very well. "You gave me one of your life crystals!" Denesia felt shy. "I promise you I will return this favor."

Years later, Ducaine and Duncan in their casino make the Peterson brothers lose everything they own, including Denesia, at the games. Ducaine, as owner of Denesia, sends Duncan to scan Denesia's form using special rays, and project it on all screens in the casino. He tells Duncan to use the software and penetrating scans to display Denesia naked on the screen. Denesia closes her eyes, and thinks of Nion. All screens in the casino, show Denesia's glowing form, she is shining so bright, that Ducaine who was watching the huge screens on the walls in blinded by the light. "What's happening with the software, Duncan debug it soon." Duncan tries, but can't figure it out. Meanwhile glowing image of Denesia on all screens condenses into tiny stars in the center of the screens, and they go supernova! They explode! All the screens in the casino shatter! Nion smiles elsewhere. He has returned the favor!"

I woke up. Now that's an in-depth detailed dream! Why did I get the feeling Andrea is going to name her kids Denesia and Nion?

The doorbell rang later in the evening. I put down my smartphone. Yes, I still keep a smartphone around. Even though I can access a lot on my watch itself, even as a light keypad springs up from my watch, I don't like the sensation of punching keys into light. Touchscreen is bad enough, as opposed to real plastic keys. Simona never understands though. She likes the light screen a lot. Anyways, I went to get the door.

I opened the door, and there stood Andrea! She had a few grey hairs, but it was definitely Andrea.

"Can I come in? I've got one hour."

I stepped aside, and she walked in. I shut the door behind me.

"Please sit down."

She sat on the couch.

"Is anyone else home?"

"No, it's just me."

"I'm Andrea, your granddaughter. You recognized me,

didn't you?"

"Yes."

"See, I have this power to time travel, every year during Christmas for an hour or so. And I dreamt that you dreamt of me showing my father Denesia's story, and were wondering about my kids."

"You dreamt that I dreamt?"

"Yes. I can't tell you too much. But since that dream I wanted to meet you. I wanted to tell you I indeed have two adopted children, who I've named Denesia and Nion! I'm so happy to be meeting you."

"I'm happy to meet you too, Andrea."

"I researched and found the address of this apartment in this time. I meditated and appeared in front of the door. Time travelling back in time can change the future. But we haven't met in the future. As yet."

"Okay, don't tell me more than you need to. Can I do anything for you?"

"Can you get me some cold milk?"

"Sure."

I went into the kitchen, grabbed the milk carton from the fridge, and poured a mug. I took it to her. She drank it, sipping and smiling at me. It reminded me of Lyceine drinking coffee on the beach that old day. I said nothing though. I smiled at Andrea.

"So, I'm just going to disappear in a few minutes."

"Okay."

"Can I get a lock of hair from you," she handed me a small scissor from her pocket.

"What for though?"

She blushed.

I cut away some of my hair, and she put it neatly into the locket she was wearing on her neck. Suddenly it occurred to me.

"You want my hair because it has DNA, right?"

"Yes, Denesia has some of Lyceine's memories. I believe she is Lyceine reincarnate. I'm going to develop your clone to a teenager, and put the electrical signals that Aaron had saved from your head. That will make your clone come alive I believe. I want you to help Denesia. She has been having some mind issues. She was searching for you on the internet for a long time. But you didn't seem to be anywhere. I'm going to bring you back for her." I was perplexed. We sat silent for some time.

"By the way, Anita and I have been committed to each other for years now. We adopted Denesia and Nion together."

"Why doesn't that surprise me?"

"Because you are clairvoyant," she had an amused expression on her face.

She took out folded pieces of paper from her pocket and

gave it to me. I took it.

"It's couple of blogs I had written about the time when I was working for years away from home. When Anita was with someone else. I met her again, she was available then, and some time afterwards we made the big decision to commit to raise children together."

She looked a little tired. But she gave me a sweet smile.

"Can you read it?"

"Now?"

"Yes, please."

I started reading,

'Lonely Saturdays.

I was walking on the side streets. Exercise good for people working sedentary jobs five days a week. It was a lovely Saturday morning. Beautiful houses lined up the streets. Roses in bloom. So many other flowers in bloom. But somehow there was no scent in the air. It was picturesque, with the mountains in the background and blue sky.

I kept walking. Brisk air hitting my face. Under a car were a very small dog and an even smaller puppy. The puppy ran up to me wagging its tail. The little dog just kept on lying there with a serious expression on his face. I watched the puppy for a little while. They didn't seem like strays. Weather was nice, they seemed happy.

So, I carried on with my walk. Someone had a garage open and people were working under the hood of a car. I walked on. I came upon an Yellow house! Never seen such a bright coloured house before. A lady was watering the garden with a hose. I waved to her, she waved back! Smile burgeoned on my face. I broke into a sprint.

A woman was on the sidewalk, trying to take a picture of her little girl on the lawn. I moved closer to her to offer to take a picture of her and her daughter. She was terror-stricken! She grabbed the little one and hurried inside.

The clouds had rolled in. Just white ones. Not heavy. I took a turn, passed a few houses that reminded me of cottages we had spent time in when we were on vacation during my childhood. Saw a locked house. Saw a young man sitting sadly on his porch who seemed vaguely familiar. I passed him by. Into a green luscious park with mown lawn and shady trees. I came upon four people so deep in sleep that they didn't stir a bit on the lawn. They were totally black from dirt. Soot black! I kept walking.

Post office passed by. I passed a public laundry room, never knew one existed there. A laundromat. I walked beyond gates into the gated-community area, and reached my apartment.

Keys unlocked the door. I put away my cell phone and wallet. I splashed some water on my face. Suddenly the apartment felt like a very lonely place. But I felt refreshed. Mornings were orange juice, bread, butter, jam and tea. Now I probably ate bananas. Made some rice. Egg curry. Took out my dark yellow vacuum cleaner and ploughed through the living space, and bedroom. I can't remember, yes, I had a

*broom that swept the kitchen. More about the apartment
later. I took the clothes in the hamper, loaded them in the
plastic green basket, and took them to the common laundry
room outside the apartment. Loaded the washer. Added
detergent. Closed lid. Chose cold water for colour wash. I
sometimes did many loads. Whites in hot water white wash.
T-shirts and night dresses in warm wash. Jeans in cold wash.
I've grown old. Don't remember the details. Sitting on the
bench in the lawn waiting for laundry to get done. Signs that
read recycled water used for the lawns, don't touch. Grabbed
mail from the mailbox. Wrote checks, put them in envelopes,
sealed them, addressed them, placed stamps on them. Placed
them for pickup at the mailbox. Filed away the bills.
Dropped the rent cheque at the lobby. Saturdays were busy
days. Washer, dryer, fold clothes, carry back, fold clothes.
Cook something for dinner. Shopping was left away for
Sundays. Let's stick to Saturdays though. Saturdays is
when a lot gets done.*

*Oh, I almost forgot. On one Saturday, I saw a dad and a
very little girl, just stepped out of the car I suppose, walking
towards their house through the lawn, with the tiny puppy
jumping for joy at the little girls' heels, followed by the small
dog! A beautiful videogram! Makes the whole Saturday
worth it."*

My dear Andrea seemed to have suffered a lot of loneliness.
I looked up from the paper, but she was gone.

I sat there quietly for a while. I continued reading the next
blog,

"The Blue Blanket

I was really late to the airport. Having cleared security, I mazed my way to the departure gate. The boarding area was completely empty, all passengers must have been boarded. There wasn't even anyone manning the gate entry door. I decided to wing it, and walk through to see if maybe the flight hadn't already taken off.

I was about to walk through, when I felt the presence of someone very near me. I turned and I think the pilot's jacket was about a few inches in front of my head. Felt like the captain himself had been hurrying. "Boarding this flight?" "Yes" "Passport please." It sounded like a captain's voice to me.

I was wearing an evening dress, don't ask how. Well, it was the only washed outfit I had when I was leaving my friend's place in a hurry. I had a school bag slung over my shoulders, which carried by to be laundered dresses, and other travelling personal effects. I was returning from my long-distance rendezvous back to where I worked for a living.

So, anyways, we were at the gate and in a hurry now. I knelt down right there, practically at the captain's feet, pulled out my passport from the bag, and handed it upwards. He perused it rather quickly. "Welcome aboard", and returning my passport walked away briskly into the gate.

I stuck my passport back into my bag, picked it up, stood up, and hurried through the gate into the interior of the plane. It seemed completely full, and then a gracious beautiful air hostess ushered me to the free seat in the front row on the aisle. I settled in tucking my bag under the seat. I was weary, and didn't realize how cold I had gotten from wearing an evening dress to the early morning five-thirty plane. The airhostess simply brought me a nice blue blanket, and covered me. It warmed me.

The plane took off. I was contemplating things numbly. Things seemed to be out of control in my life. I was just drifting along wherever life was taking me. Long distance relationships, the daily office routines. Then, the plane was landing. There were some announcements that we had to do some kind of pitstop for weather or fuel, I don't really remember. The plane sat there for a while. Our arrival was going to be delayed. I was wondering if I should call office and tell them I was getting delayed.

The crew opened the plane doors. I remember getting up and walking to the rear door, and stepping out. There was just another crew member at the exit. Everyone else was content with sitting it out in their seats. Outside, I could see our plane was parked in a remote airport. Could see a road off on to one side with little traffic. In front of me though where A-shaped hills, live peaceful green, looming in a lonely background. The breeze was cool, and the clouds were fogging the sky. I went back to my seat.

After a while, I went through the front door back to the outside. Standing on the landing, at the top of the steps. I felt someone nearby. I was numb, inertia was I. With what life was to me, I was just a soft log being carried along by the current. I became aware of the captain's jacket. Probably he was out for some air too. He must have been there for a minute or so. Must have sensed my mind was in an appeased state with the green scene, and felt my state didn't need disturbing. He left quietly.

I lingered a few more moments, and went back to my seat.

The plane took off. It seemed like a very gentle flight. We landed. I picked up my bag. The blue blanket was wrapped like a shawl around me now, although I was oblivious. I walked out, felt the breeze again, took a cab and came home. Then, I realized I had brought the blue blanket with me."

15 ALL OF US TOGETHER

We were out for a picnic in a remote hill outside the city –
Simona, Pierre, Lyceine and me. We had a blanket spread
out, and the picnic hamper opened. Lyceine has packed
croissants, apple tarts, lemon cakes and bananas among
other things. Birds were chirping softly. I had brought our
boombox, and played slow music on it. Simona was slow
dancing with Pierre. I was just lazing on the blanket.
Lyceine had gone to tinkle in the woods, when it happened.
Tristan's ship materialized out of nowhere in the sky.
Simona sensed the computers on the ship, "He's preparing
to fire on us!" Next second was pure horror.

I felt I was drowning in the waters. I swam up hard, and
looked around. I saw Lyceine swim up to Pierre, grab him
and vanish. I turned and scanned the waters. I saw Andrea
grab Aaron and vanish! Where was Simona? "Simona!"
"Dad!" She was behind me. Thank God she's okay! "Let's
go to the green planet!" "Okay."

Everything was quiet on the green planet. The green meadows stretched on one side as far as the eye could see.

"What about Pierre and Mom?"

"Mom used the teleporter watch I had made for her to get them both safely out of the way. They are out there somewhere. I'm going to see what happened, okay?"

"Yeah, sure."

I closed my eyes and tried moving my mind in the reverse. But my mind wanted to go into the future for some reason.

Andrea was dreaming about the bomb blast, and woke up. It was only June. She was talking to herself, "Six months till Christmas. It's only a month since Paul and Denesia's wedding. Maybe their union is what has triggered this dream. I have to talk to Aaron." She called Aaron, but Aaron didn't answer the call.

I was straining. I was tired. I let it go, and opened my eyes. Simona was texting using her watch.

"Mom sends message that she and Pierre are home."

"You opened a channel across alternate universes?"

"You were doing your mind thing. I felt very worried. So, I worked the watch to open a channel and sent mom a message that we're on the green planet. She responded immediately."

"Close the channel now Simona. We should never have left the city for the picnic. Tristan's been watching us all the time."

"I'm closing it right now, Dad."

I closed my eyes again and went into the future. Why wasn't Aaron picking up the phone call? Aaron was lying on his bed thinking. He looked very thin like he hadn't eaten in a long time. His hair was unkempt and he had quite a beard grown.

I tried to rewind time in my mind a little bit.

Aaron was driving his car happily, when the car ahead braked suddenly. He hit the brakes quickly too. Soon the cars stopped. Aaron got out, and walked ahead to see what was happening. A young man's body was on the middle of the road. He looked pretty hurt. It looked like someone had hit him, and driven by. The young woman, driver of the other car, fainted. Aaron caught her, and laid her aside carefully. And then he set to fixing and healing the young man. But, no matter how he tried, he couldn't get him to heal. No light flowed from his hands. Life drained out of the young man. It tormented Aaron.

I opened my eyes. This event really affected Aaron a lot. This explains his descent into depression – inattention to himself and the phones.

I reached with my mind again.

Andrea was taking care of Aaron, pep-talking him, "Aaron, you can do it. I believe if the need arose your healing power will come back to you. Maybe the young man you were trying to heal didn't want to come back, maybe his grip on his life was not so strong. Aaron, its Christmas today, the day I get to time travel. I have to tell you that somewhere in the past our family got bombed! Mum and Dad were not married then. But you and I exist. This means that they have to be saved. I firmly believe that it's you who can save them. We've got this day today, again it will only be next year that I can time travel. I'm going to take you to the time after the bomb blast. You have to try to save them, okay?"

Andrea held on to Aaron's hands, and concentrated with her mind. Aaron and Andrea arrived on the blast scene. The picnic spot had been beside a dam. "Aaron, that Dam might break, I think. The blast must have affected it." "Time pressure, thank you sis!" Aaron went to work. It was a pretty bad scene. But he focused his thoughts, and light flowed from his hands. "I need you. I need all of you!" All scattered charred tissues gathered together, and formed the bodies, and wandering souls got restored to them. They were just waking, when the dam cracked!

I opened my eyes, and said to Simona, "We had help Simona, we had help. That's how we are alive today."

16 AND THEN

I was sitting at my desk by myself. I had nothing to do just then. I thought about looking into the future or the past. I tried, but my mind drew a blank.

 Simona walked in, "Dad, shouldn't you be finding out about Tristan?"

"Your mom gets stressed if I talk about Tristan. She is very sensitive to the topic, and doesn't like to talk about the past much."

"And you can't see about Tristan?"

"The seeing thing seems like it only works with dear ones. I can't see anything about Tristan. Also, I can't always see at will, Simona. It comes to effect only when it is absolutely necessary for me or something like that."

"I know Dad. It's the same thing with me. I can't understand electrical signals all the time at will."

Simona had gone to meet Pierre. The day was over. The sun had set.

"Lyceine, tell me about Tristan."

"I'll give you the highlights. Tristan had a twin brother, who stole Tristan's girl, and tried to poison Tristan, I think. This twin died later. Tristan tried to help this girl, but she refused Tristan's help. Tristan had been in love with her for a long time. But she shut Tristan out. Wouldn't talk to him, or see him. Tristan loved her very much. I think she loved Tristan too, but there was something stopping her. Tristan liked to be quiet and by himself, but his father kept pushing him to be actively involved in politics. Tristan was a natural orator, and the crowds loved to hear him. Tristan needed time to think alone, but his father kept interfering with his reverie. One day, Tristan was on edge, he was practising gun shooting. His father said something about him and his hobbies, and that his brother was a thousand times better than him. Something broke within Tristan. He shot his father in the arm. The next second he regretted it. He was so confused, and in anguish, it didn't help him at all. His mind degenerated a lot brooding over the incident. He lashed out at anyone who questioned his authority on anything. Zircov and Tristan had a common interest in exploring new technologies. I think Zircov was helping Tristan travel to alternate universes a lot. One day we got information that Tristan's enemies are planning a trap for him on a certain universe that he frequented. Tristan was missing. Zircov sent me to find him. I fount you instead. I don't know what was in the box from the mansion. Tristan told me killing people in our universe sent them back to the universe they came from. I was supposed to protect him that day, he was so vulnerable, but he got hit, it was my fault. Tristan became paranoid, he got visions that his brother was trying to kill him, and visions of a prophecy that a little girl would end him. Zircov was killed. Tristan had enemies. I read Zircov's letter to me on his computer. He said that Tristan should be assassinated, as he was trying to scan universes for people to be exterminated. I shared this info with the guidance council and they informed me that Tristan should be assassinated." Lyceine was tired.

Tristan and I were engaged in a vicious cycle, one trying to kill the other because one thought the other was trying to kill the one.

That night I dreamed that Evola finally reached out to Tristan, and that Tristan had become a better person.

17 THE WOMAN IN THE BLUE DRESS VIII

I woke up. Lyceine was standing beside the bed in her favorite blue dress.

 I said, "I just had the most elaborate dream, Lyceine. And I truly believe it will come to pass."

Lyceine, "What was it about?"

Me, "It's about our family tree! And our next life."

Lyceine, "Tell me more'"

"But it's slipping my mind. You know how sometime you wake up from a dream, and all the details are blurring away in the present?"

"Yes."

"Something like that is happening."

"Well, don't fight it. It will come to you."

"I know."

"It maybe for the best. Sometimes you have to forget the dream to live it!"

I let it go and buried my head gently into her stomach area. I could feel the baby move inside. "Are you dreaming baby?"

18 THE WOMAN IN THE BLUE DRESS
IX

Lyceine was saying to me, "I believe that, all that is in existence, all the multiverses came from one consciousness. We come from and return to it. So, it's only natural that we keep discovering conduits to each other in different ways and different forms. We are all more connected to each other than we know."

I woke up. My hand's radiator burn has been healing. My dream is slipping from my mind. I vaguely remember Lyceine's advice not to fight it. I'm ready to wake up to life. If you're wondering how my life is going to be, go read the title of the book.

Now, it's time for you to wake up from this story too.

Go dream your own dreams, and live your own story!

19 IN PEACE I

Since you are continuing to read this book, I'll tell you what happened after I dreamt that Evola reached out to Tristan.

Pierre was very impressed with the teleport watch I had designed for Lyceine. "How does this work?" Pierre asked. I said," Well, currently I've programmed it such that no matter where Lyceine is, if she presses 0033 on the watch it teleports Lyceine back to our hobby room in the house. When I designed it at first, it allowed teleports out, but we didn't know where she ended up. Although it was somewhere within the space net." Pierre said, "Fascinating."

Pierre was very interested. So, I explained to Pierre some details of how I had constructed the teleporter watch. In the days that followed Pierre spent time with me in our hobby room. Often Simona walked in with mugs of coffee for us, and she would stand behind Pierre, put her hand on his shoulder, and listen in on our discussions. Lyceine sometimes was with us too. She would tousle Pierre's hair when he was frustrated that he couldn't follow what I was saying. Pierre didn't mind these favorite displays of affection by the women at all. He was all smiles.

One day Pierre said, "How about we create another watch for Simona so she can teleport to my apartment. And another watch so I can teleport here?" I didn't scare him by telling him that Simona could teleport at will yet. Pierre seemed to fully realize though that by his proposal, what he was applying to was free entry into our house. He was to become a member of the household. I was in effect giving him keys to the front door of the house. I looked at Simona, "Are you ready for this?" Simona nodded. So did Lyceine.

So, we set to work, and in a few weeks succeeded in creating the two watches. Simona and Pierre used it generously.

Next, Pierre came up with the idea to create a programmable teleporter watch. So, what we did was create this technology, and Pierre tested it out. We went to the living room, Pierre marked an X on the wall, and wrote teleport location on it, turned around and recorded this location as 0050 on the programmable watch. I watched with interest standing beside Pierre. He then punched 0033 into the watch, and zapped. In a minute he appeared back. Pierre said, "I punched 0050 from the hobby room, and I'm back here!"

Pierre made Simona stand in the teleport location, under the X, in the living room. He stood by the couch and tried teleporting using 0050. The watch refused to teleport him. Simona moved out of the way, and then Pierre tried 0050, and it worked again! Pierre kissed Simona out of joy.

We discussed space net technology, and developed a short-range teleporter shield, that covered a house, or a building – a mini space net. You could teleport into the house only if you were previously registered with the shield generator.

Pierre said, "I think we can mass manufacture the programmable teleporter watches and shield generators, and make it available to the public. This way we can reduce traffic on the roads!"

I said, "We could do that. But, there's a catch. I don't know what side-effects would manifest in our bodies if we teleported often."

Pierre said, "How about this. We will first start with watches pre-programmed with ten locations – specific beaches, lakes, waterfalls, National Parks. We will get them out with a disclaimer, 'Try at your own risk'. This way we get people to test them out. We will study the effects of teleportation on these people, and then decide how we want to go about it. I suspect many people will experience dizziness and nausea. But eventually it may be worth the effort. People never stop travelling by plane because they get jetlag. Or avoid ships altogether because of sea-sickness. There are a class of people who become pilots, and a class of people who become sailors. There will be a class of people who teleport."

Pierre was so optimistic. It caught on to me. I said, "Let's work on our manufacturing project then. We will start with designing the manufacturing process. It might take us months, I reckon."

20 IN PEACE II

It was a quiet day. Simona and Pierre weren't around. Lyceine said to me, "Pierre is so excited about teleport technology. But the truth is, once you've done it, it loses its charm. It is just another experience. There is so much more to life than teleports."

"Yes, but I approve of him trying to put it to use for the betterment of everyone."

"But the watch works by deriving power from Zircov's crystals. You've read Zircov's documentations. And used the crystals."

"I've found a way to grow these crystals Lyceine. I've been meaning to tell you that for some time."

"I've been wondering though, how come nobody has invented teleportation yet."

"Its possible others have, and we don't know. It's also

possible that even though I've shut down pathways to other universes, someone might have a workaround to bypass it. But the chances are slim at best. Nothing is completely certain, Lyceine. But we create a world where we can live with some certainty, and live within it. The possibility of change, that's what makes life interesting. Let's put it this way. You eat an apple, you don't really know who made it, but you eat it because you want to, and you are ready to face the consequences. Most likely it has side-effects, but we take risks. There is hope that the creator of the apple will come to our aid when something goes wrong, and that the creator's creator is helping him. At best, there is hope in infinity."

"If you put the watch out there, people are bound to discover the crystal, ask questions, and grow them like you did, and so on."

"Yes, that's possible. We will have to have faith in humanity."

"You do realize that you may have to divulge your travels to other universes, and possibly be forced to open up the pathways to everyone."

"Ah, in time Lyceine. Everything takes time. It's also possible people lose interest in teleportation. Once, Tristan got back with Evola, Tristan stopped univporting and teleporting around, and settled down with her, didn't he?"

"Yes, he is doing well in administration, and writing and delivering fabulous speeches. Evola texts me through the channel that you let Simona open. It's one bridge we've left open between our universes."

"We can't sever all ties. It's good to keep bridges. It comes with responsibilities, of course. We are in some fashion ambassadors between universes."

21 IN PEACE III

We were silent for a while.

"Evola wrote to me about what Tristan has been telling her. He put Simona in the incinerator, and closed the doors, and was watching her on screen, watching what she was doing. She was just sitting there with her eyes closed. She looked so innocent and fragile to him. He couldn't bring himself to push the button, and before he knew it, she disappeared from the incinerator. Also, when Tristan found us on the picnic spot, he was preparing to fire, letting his anger flow out, threatening you and Simona, but he couldn't bring himself to push the button finally. But something happened, his ship fired without his command."

"Do you believe this, Lyceine?"

"I do believe him. I've always believed in Tristan."

"But you helped assassinate him!"

"Zircov made a pretty strong accusation. I delivered his views to the council. The council did its research, and found Tristan unstable, and ordered the assassination. I followed orders. We were hunting Tristan down under my leadership. Tristan got wind of things. When we attacked fortress after fortress trying to find Tristan, using you to gain access through biological barriers, and our people combating Tristan's people, instead of carrying the instant killing poison gun that the council had given me, I carried a gun which used a certain liquid that Zircov had given me when I went searching for Tristan. Zircov had said to me, 'if you find yourself in an inescapable situation, and your watch is damaged, take this liquid and it will make you appear dead for a few hours, and then zap you to an alternate universe.' I remember saying to Zircov laughingly, 'I will zap provided no one burns my body by then!' So, anyways I used that liquid to kill Tristan. I wanted to give him a chance. We buried him, but he zapped out."

"Now that's something I didn't guess!"

"Are you mad?"

"No, not at all. So, when we were disappearing out of plum jam, you had some idea of what could be happening. And Tristan being there."

"It all happened so fast. And I was really tired."

"But you saw Tristan take away your watch and leave us in the dynamite site. We could have died! You were ready to sacrifice yourself and me. You could have explained things to me."

"I really trusted Tristan. I don't think that was any dynamite near us. He was bluffing. He likes to bluff a lot with his friends. But never in his speeches."

"Was I the dummy?"

"No, you were the purest of heart I have ever known."

"I threw a knife at him Lyceine, that killed him, and caused him to zap!"

"In self-defense. I love you so much. I was always with you after the assassination. And I never let you out of space net alone much. Still Tristan's friends got to you. That's when I was really scared. I was beginning to worry that Zircov's opinion might not have been baseless." She looked horrified.

"So, Tristan's in the grey area. I think I understand why you kept things to yourself. It was very difficult for you. I never asked you questions and trusted you implicitly. You didn't want to ruin the pristine time you spent with me."

I sighed. I smiled at her, and then I remembered.

"It still remains that someone fired on us. So, there's evil out there but we can't tell what or how. But thankfully there's been so many good things happening in our life. Good and evil are at loggerheads all the time. Meanwhile, we have to live our lives, as best as we can."

"That makes me nervous."

"But Lyceine, there is a natural order to things. Doesn't the earth revolve around the sun steadily. There is so much order in the universes."

"Yes, my heart revolves around you. I'm glad things sort themselves out every now and then."

I was thinking.

"Paul, why won't you hold my hand?"

I looked down, and I saw Lyceine had put her hand in mine.

"My hand had gone numb Lyceine. Yesterday it was just my fingers, now it's my whole hand. I think I touched the crystal accidentally, even though I was very careful. That crystal is supposed to be very cold."

Lyceine was visibly alarmed.

"What do we do?"

"Zircov mentions there is the opposite – warm crystals. We need to find them. They're probably the anti-dote."

"We've got to talk to Tristan about this. I want you to open a channel, and we are going to meet him. We'll find the warm crystals, whichever planet or universe they may be in."

She was close to tears.

Don't worry reader, we found the warm crystals eventually. But that is another story!